Friends for Never

by Nancy Krulik • illustrated by John & Wendy

Grosset & Dunlap

For Isabelle and Ian Gale— makers of
rainbows, with insatiable imaginations!—N.K.

For Eric—true friends for EVER!—J&W

Text copyright © 2004 by Nancy Krulik. Illustrations copyright © 2004 by
John and Wendy. All rights reserved. Published by Grosset & Dunlap, a
division of Penguin Young Readers Group, 345 Hudson Street, New York,
New York 10014. GROSSET & DUNLAP is a trademark of Penguin Group
(USA) Inc. Printed in the U.S.A.

Library of Congress Cataloging-in-Publication Data

Krulik, Nancy E.

Friends for never / by Nancy Krulik ; illustrated by John & Wendy.

p. cm. — (Katie Kazoo, switcheroo ; 14)
Summary: Snubbed by her best friend Suzanne, Katie magically turns into
her as she is making her modelling debut at a fashion show at the mall.
Includes a recipe for fruit salad.
ISBN 0-448-43606-X (pbk.)
[1. Models (Persons)—Fiction. 2. Best friends—Fiction. 3. Friendship—
Fiction. 4. Schools—Fiction. 5. Magic—Fiction.] I. John & Wendy. II.
Title. III. Series.

PZ7.K944Ft 2004
[Fic]—dc22   2004009203

ISBN 0-448-43606-X   10 9 8 7

Chapter 1

"Yodel-ay-hee-hoo!" Katie Carew shouted. "Yodel-ay-hee-hoo!"

"That was perfect!" her teacher, Mr. Guthrie, congratulated her. "You sounded like a real native of Switzerland."

Katie blushed. She wasn't usually the type of kid to yodel in front of her whole class. But that was the kind of thing you did when you were in Mr. Guthrie's fourth-grade class.

Mr. Guthrie wasn't a typical teacher. He did things his own way.

Like now. The kids were studying world geography. But rather than just reading about Switzerland, the kids in class 4A were standing on a hill in the field behind the school, practicing yodeling. The hill was the closest thing the elementary school had to the mountains of Switzerland. Mr. Guthrie called it the Cherrydale Alps.

"Who's next?" Mr. Guthrie asked.

"Oh, oh, oh!" Kadeem Carter raised his hand really high. "My turn! Please, Mr. G.!"

Mr. Guthrie laughed. "Okay, Kadeem, let's hear *your* best yodel."

"YODEL-AY-HE-HOOOOOOOOOOOOO!"

Katie covered her ears. So did a lot of the other kids. Kadeem was really loud.

Mr. Guthrie smiled. "That was definitely the yodel to beat all yodels."

Kadeem bowed to the class. "Thank you, thank you!" he said.

Katie rolled her eyes. Kadeem was always joking around.

"Okay, since nothing's going to top that, let's head back into the building," Mr. Guthrie said. "We have just enough time before lunch

to take a surprise math quiz."

"Ugh," the kids groaned. They hated
surprise quizzes.

Katie sighed. Sometimes Mr. Guthrie
could be just like any other teacher.

Katie walked into her classroom, plopped
down into her beanbag, and got ready to take

the quiz. The kids in 4A all sat in beanbag chairs. Mr. Guthrie thought kids learned better when they were comfortable.

The kids were very proud of their bean-bags. They spent a lot of time decorating them. The decorations reflected what the class was learning about.

When the class had been studying birds, the kids had all turned the beanbags into giant nests. When they had been learning about American history, the kids had used construction paper, glue, and cardboard to create historical scenes on their beanbags.

Right now, class 4A's world geography unit was Europe. Katie had used black pipe cleaners to build the Eiffel Tower from France on her beanbag. Her pal Emma Weber had constructed the London Bridge out of cardboard.

Emma Stavros had decorated her beanbag with pictures of funny-looking trolls from Norway.

Andrew Epstein's beanbag was the scariest one. He'd used cardboard and black construction paper to build a dark castle. His beanbag was supposed to be Dracula's home in Romania. There was even a picture of a vampire on the top of the castle.

George Brennan's beanbag was really goofy. He'd used lots of Styrofoam cups to build Italy's Leaning Tower of Pisa. In real life, that tower tilted a little to one side. On George's beanbag, the tower leaned so far over, it hit the floor. He was constantly gluing the cups back together.

Kadeem had a funny beanbag, too. He'd used brown cloth pillowcases stuffed with cotton to make a giant hot-dog bun around his red beanbag. He said it was a German frankfurter.

"Hey, Kadeem and Andrew," George called out. "You guys know what Dracula's favorite snack is?"

Kadeem shook his head.

"A fang-furter!" George said. He laughed at his own joke.

Kadeem couldn't let George be the only funny one. "What do you call a slice of dessert in Italy?" he asked.

"What?" George wondered.

"A pizza pie!"

Katie giggled. She really liked when George and Kadeem tried to out-joke each other. Mr. Guthrie called it having a joke-off.

"Wow," Mr. Guthrie exclaimed. "It's an international joke-off! Those were good ones, guys."

"Good enough to get us out of that math quiz?" George asked hopefully.

"Not a chance."

As Mr. Guthrie went to his filing cabinet to get the quiz, Katie thought about life in class 4A. Sure, they had to do regular work, like this quiz. But they also did a lot of really great stuff, like yodeling and telling jokes.

And the kids in class 4A were the only

ones in the whole school to have a *snake* for a class pet. No hamster, guinea pig, or turtle could *ever* be as cool as Slinky the Snake!

It was hard to believe that Katie had ever wanted to be in class 4B with Ms. Sweet. Not that Ms. Sweet wasn't a nice teacher. She was. But Mr. Guthrie was a lot cooler.

Then again, Katie's two best friends, Jeremy Fox and Suzanne Lock, were in class 4B. Katie missed them sometimes. It would have been nice to be with them all day.

But Katie still got to see Suzanne and Jeremy at recess, during track team practices, and on the weekends after her Saturday morning clarinet lessons. They still had lots of fun together.

Katie had learned something really important in fourth grade. She didn't have to be with her best friends all day long. No matter what class they were in, Katie and her pals were *friends forever*!

Chapter 2

"Hey, Katie," Emma W. called as Katie walked out onto the playground after lunch. "You want to jump rope with Mandy and me?"

"Sure," Katie agreed happily. "Just let me find Suzanne. She's probably with Jessica. We can all play."

Katie knew Emma W. would like it if they all played together. Last year, when Emma was in class 3B, Jessica had been her best friend. But this year, they were in different classes. Emma didn't get to hang out with Jessica all the time anymore.

"Okay," Emma W. said. "But hurry up. I

have a new rhyme I want to try."

Katie looked around the playground for Suzanne and Jessica. She found them standing next to the big oak tree.

"Hi, you guys," Katie said as she approached Suzanne and Jessica. "Wanna jump rope with Emma W., Mandy, and me?"

Suzanne sighed. "Jump rope?" she asked. "Are you kidding?"

Katie seemed surprised. "Kidding?"

"We don't do that kind of stuff," Suzanne declared. Jessica nodded in agreement.

"But you jumped rope all the time last year," Katie reminded Suzanne.

"Exactly," Suzanne replied. "In *third* grade. But we're in fourth grade now. Jumping rope is for babies."

"Oh," Katie said. She felt embarrassed. She hadn't thought of it that way. "So what are you guys going to do?"

"Just hang out here and talk," Suzanne replied.

Katie frowned. She had to get back to where Emma and Mandy were waiting for her. They needed at least three people to play jump rope. "I don't really have time to talk," she said.

"That's okay," Suzanne replied. "Our conversation is private anyway."

Katie couldn't believe it! Suzanne, *her best friend*, was telling her to go away. She glared at Suzanne.

"Don't look so angry," Suzanne told her. "It's not about you. It's about my modeling class."

"What's so private about that?" Katie asked her. "Everyone knows you're taking a modeling class."

"Yes, but she's my new assistant." Suzanne pointed to Jessica.

"Your *what*?"

"I'm going to need an assistant when I'm a famous model," Suzanne explained to Katie. "So I have to teach her all about modeling stuff. That's what we're talking about. We've started a modeling club."

"What kind of stuff do you do in a modeling club?" Katie asked.

"Oh, you know, talk about new hairstyles and lip glosses." Suzanne stuck out her bottom lip. "I'm wearing grape gloss with glitter."

"Oh, I thought you ate a purple Popsicle at lunch," Katie said.

Suzanne rolled her eyes. "That's why *you're* not my assistant," she said.

"That was really mean, Suzanne," Katie replied.

Suzanne paused for a moment. "Oh, I guess I forgot to tell you . . ." she began.

"Tell me what?"

"My name's not Suzanne anymore."

Katie stared at her. "Excuse me?"

"Suzanne is too plain a name for someone like me. So I gave myself a new one. Now my name is Ocean. That's *much* more sophisticated."

Katie started to laugh. Suzanne had done some pretty weird things, but this was one of the weirdest! She looked over at Jessica. "What's *your* name? Sand?"

"Her name is *River*," Suzanne said. "I came up with it."

Jessica nodded. "Now we're Ocean and River."

"Water names, get it?" Suzanne added.

Katie looked at Ocean and River. They were in the same class. They'd given themselves new names. And they were in a club together—a club they had not asked Katie to join! They were acting like . . . *best friends*!

Katie knew she should get back to Mandy and Emma, but she didn't want to be left out by Suzanne and Jessica either. "Do you think

I should get a new name, too?" she asked. "I could be Sea or Waterfall or something."

Suzanne shook her head. "Plain old Katie fits you just fine. *You* don't need a sophisticated name."

Katie wasn't jealous anymore. Now she was just mad. "I'm not plain!" she exclaimed. "I'm as sophisticated as you are!"

Suzanne looked at Katie's red high-top sneakers and jeans. Then she studied her own black-and-white cowboy boots and short denim skirt. "Oh, Katie," she said. "Don't be silly. You're not sophisticated. You're just Katie."

Katie scowled.

"All the people in class 4A are pretty much like you," Suzanne continued. "You fit in just fine there. So it's okay."

Katie turned on her heels and stormed off. She wasn't going to talk to Suzanne about this anymore. *It wasn't okay*. Not at all!

Chapter 3

That afternoon, Katie walked home from school all by herself. Emma W. had to help her mother take her little brothers for haircuts. Jeremy had a drum lesson. And *Ocean* was hanging out with River.

Katie felt really alone. She started to think about how things were in third grade—*back when she and Suzanne did things together.*

"I wish . . ." she began. Then she stopped herself, quick. Katie knew better than to wish for things. Wishes sometimes came true. And that could cause big problems.

It had all started one day at the beginning of third grade. Katie had lost the football

game for her team, ruined her favorite pair of
pants, and let out a big burp in front of the
whole class. It was the worst day of Katie's
life. That night, Katie had wished she could
be anyone but herself.

There must have been a shooting star over-
head when she made that wish, because the
very next day the magic wind came.

The magic wind felt like a wild tornado.
But this wind blew just around Katie. It was
so powerful that every time it came, it turned
her into somebody else! Katie never knew
when the wind would arrive. But whenever
it did, her whole world was turned upside
down . . . switcheroo!

The first time the magic wind came, it had
turned Katie into Speedy, class 3A's hamster!
That morning, Katie had escaped from the
hamster cage and wound up in the boys'
locker room! Luckily, Katie switched back
into herself before any of the boys could tell
she was running around wearing nothing but

Speedy's fur coat.

The magic wind came back again and again after that. It had turned her into Lucille the lunch lady, Principal Kane, and even Katie's third-grade teacher, mean old Mrs. Derkman! One time, the wind switcherooed Katie into her science camp counselor, Genie the Meanie. That time, she'd gotten all her friends lost in the woods!

The wind had also changed Katie into other kids—like Emma W. and Suzanne's baby sister, Heather. One time, the wind had switcherooed her into Jeremy, and Katie had started a huge fight between all the girls and boys in her grade.

Another time, the magic wind had turned Katie into her very own dog, Pepper. She'd gotten into an argument with a squirrel and destroyed her next-door neighbor's garden. Considering the fact that Katie's next-door neighbor was Mrs. Derkman, it had been really awful.

Katie never knew who the magic wind was going to change her into next. But she did know one thing. She wasn't ever going to make another wish, ever again. Wishes didn't always turn out the way you expected them to.

Chapter 4

The next morning, when Katie got to school, she spotted Suzanne walking back and forth in front of a tree. Her back was really straight and her neck was stretched up long, like a swan's. She looked kind of weird.

At first, Katie didn't want to go over and talk to Suzanne. She was still kind of mad at her about the day before.

Then she thought about it for a moment. She and Suzanne had been in fights before. But they always made up. Katie was pretty sure that Suzanne would be sorry about how she'd treated her yesterday. She would surely ask her to join the modeling club today.

Katie decided to give Suzanne another chance. That was the kind of thing best friends did for each other.

"Hi, Suzanne," Katie greeted her.

"*Ocean,*" Suzanne reminded Katie.

"Oh, yeah. Ocean. Hi."

"Hi." Suzanne kept on walking back and forth.

"What are you doing?"

"Practicing walking."

Katie looked at her strangely. "You've been walking since you were two."

Suzanne rolled her eyes and sighed. "I'm practicing walking on a *runway*, Katie," she explained. "I have a big modeling show coming up, remember?"

Katie nodded. "I think you walk really nicely," she assured Suzanne.

Suzanne frowned.

"*Nicely* isn't good enough. I have to be perfect. I want to be the model everyone remembers!"

At just that moment, Emma Stavros came running over to the girls. She was wearing a huge silver medal around her neck.

"Wow! Where'd you get that?" Katie asked. She was really impressed.

"At the ice-skating competitions yesterday. I took second place in figure skating!" Emma sounded really proud of herself.

Suzanne stopped walking and looked at Emma. "Only *second* place," Suzanne sniffed.

"Well, the first-place winner was a *sixth*-grader," Emma said with a shrug.

"Second place is awesome," Katie assured her. "And your medal is so cool! I've never seen one that big!"

"Thanks," Emma said with a smile. "Oh, look, there's Mandy. I've got to show it to her!"

"What a show-off," Suzanne said as Emma raced off toward Mandy.

Katie tried really hard not to laugh.

Imagine Suzanne calling someone *else* a show-off. "She's just proud. She should be. That's an amazing medal."

"It's tacky and ugly," Suzanne argued.

"That's what you say," Katie told her. "*I* think it's really cool."

"You don't know *anything* about accessories," Suzanne replied. "Someone as small as Emma S. should never wear a big silver medal around her neck."

Katie looked at her strangely. "What are you talking about?"

"*Accessories.* You know—necklaces, earrings, scarves," Suzanne explained. "I'm an expert on accessories. We're studying them in modeling school now."

Katie was getting tired of hearing about modeling.

But Suzanne wasn't finished talking about it. She looked Katie up and down, and then frowned. "You know, now that we're not in the same class, you don't dress as well as you used to."

Katie looked down at her black running pants and zebra-striped sweater. She liked the way she looked. "What's wrong with what I'm wearing?"

"It's the animal print," Suzanne told her. "That's *so* last year. This year, people are wearing different kinds of patterns. See?" She pointed to the pink, green, and yellow polka-dot shirt she was wearing.

Before Katie could reply, Jessica came walking over. "Hi, Ocean," she greeted Suzanne. "Hi, Katie."

"Hi, River," Suzanne said with a smile. Then she turned back to Katie. "You see the plaid skirt River's wearing? That's the kind of pattern I mean."

"Ocean helped me pick it out," Jessica

explained to Katie. "Our modeling club went on a field trip to the mall."

"We had fun, didn't we?" Suzanne asked Jessica. The girls giggled together.

Katie scowled. Obviously, Suzanne wasn't going to ask her to join their club after all.

"Did you bring the orange lip gloss?" Suzanne asked Jessica.

Jessica nodded. "And your round brush, too. Now you'll be able to fix your makeup and hair all day long."

Suzanne sighed heavily. "It's so much pressure being a model. I have to be gorgeous all the time."

Ugh! Katie couldn't stand listening to Suzanne's bragging anymore. She turned and walked away without even saying good-bye.

Ocean and River didn't even seem to notice she'd gone.

Chapter 5

That afternoon, Katie and Emma W. walked home with Jeremy. As they left the school yard, Katie saw Jessica and Suzanne standing by themselves, giggling about something.

Katie frowned. "Those two are getting to be real snobs," Katie moaned.

"Getting to be?" Jeremy said. "Katie, Suzanne's always thought she was better than everyone else."

Katie sighed. She guessed that was true.

"She's *your* best friend, not mine," Jeremy reminded her.

Katie sighed again. These days, Suzanne

wasn't acting like she was Katie's best friend, either. "You know," she said slowly, "*we* could start a club. The three of us could be the first members."

"What kind of club?" Jeremy and Emma asked at once.

"Well, you guys know I take cooking classes on Wednesdays, right?" Katie asked.

Emma and Jeremy nodded.

"I know lots of great recipes now," Katie continued. "We could start a cooking club. I know my mom would let us meet in my kitchen."

"That sounds good," Jeremy agreed.

"It sounds *delicious*," Emma added.

"We could ask all our friends to join," Katie said. "Especially the ones who like to eat. We could meet Saturday afternoons, right after my clarinet lesson."

"We have to ask George, for sure," Jeremy said. "He'll eat anything. And Kevin will come if we're making something with tomatoes."

"He ate twenty-seven of those grape tomatoes at lunch today," Emma added. "I thought he was going to be sick."

"Not the tomato king," Katie assured her. "Kevin's eaten more than that before." She thought for a minute. "We should probably ask Mandy, Zoe, and Miriam, too."

"How about Manny?" Jeremy said.

"Sure," Katie agreed. "And Becky . . ."

"Do we have to ask *her*?" Jeremy interrupted. "She makes me nuts."

Katie laughed. Becky Stern had a big crush on Jeremy. She flirted with him all the time. He hated it.

"I think we should invite everyone," Katie said. Then she looked back to where Suzanne and Jessica were huddled together, talking. "Well, *almost* everyone," she corrected herself.

Chapter 6

"Please pass the applesauce," Katie asked Mandy. She put a slice of cheese on top of each of her slices of bread.

It was Saturday afternoon. Katie, Mandy, George, Jeremy, Emma W., and Manny were all gathered in Katie's kitchen. They were making applesauce recipes from the recipe Katie had gotten in her Wednesday afternoon cooking class.

"This is a great idea," George said as he poured a heaping spoonful of cinnamon and sugar over the applesauce that he had plopped on a slice of bread. Then he put another slice of bread on top to make a sandwich and covered it with a slice of American cheese. "Here you go, Mrs. Carew."

Katie's mother laughed as she popped George's cheese, applesauce, and cinnamon sugar sandwich into the oven. "That's your *third* sandwich, George," she remarked. "You must really like these."

"I love when the cheese gets gooey in the oven," he replied. "And the way the cinnamon and sugar gets all syrupy. Yum!"

"Oops!" Emma W. exclaimed. A big blob of applesauce had fallen on the floor. "I'm sorry, Mrs. Carew."

"Don't worry about it," Katie assured her friend. "Our cleanup crew will get it."

Sure enough, Pepper, Katie's cocker spaniel, padded over and began licking the applesauce off the floor.

"That dog will eat anything, Katie Kazoo!" George exclaimed, using the super-cool nickname he'd given her.

"Look who's talking," Jeremy said.

"George, I saw you put hot sauce on a tuna fish sandwich the other day. *Blech*!"

"I love hot sauce," George boasted. "The hotter the better. I'll eat it on anything."

"Even these applesauce and cheese sandwiches?" Manny asked.

George frowned. "Okay, well, maybe not *any*thing," he admitted.

Manny turned to Katie. "I'm going to start a database of all our recipes," he told her. "What do you think we should call these?"

Katie thought for a minute. Her friends all seemed really happy making the sandwiches. That gave her an idea. "How about Apple-y Ever After Sandwiches?"

"Perfect," Manny said. He took a pen from his pocket and wrote that down on the top of his hand. Manny was always writing things on his hands. That way, he never forgot anything—at least not until he took a shower.

"Katie, I can't believe you didn't ask Suzanne to join this club," Mandy said between bites of her Apple-y Ever After Sandwich. "You guys always do things like this together."

"Not anymore," Katie replied.

"But you invited everyone else in our grade to join the club," Manny reminded her.

"Not everyone," Emma W. corrected him. "We didn't ask Jessica, either."

"They're too busy with their dumb old modeling club to do anything with us," Jeremy added.

"Look at me . . . I'm a model," George said. He wiggled his hips wildly, pretending to walk up and down a fashion runway.

The kids all laughed. At first, Katie felt kind of bad about the way George was making fun of Suzanne. Especially since she wasn't there to defend herself.

But then Katie remembered *why* Suzanne wasn't there.

"Aren't you and Suzanne friends anymore?" Mandy asked. She took a big bite of her gooey applesauce sandwich.

Katie shrugged. "I guess not. She and Jessica, I mean *River*, do everything together now."

"But I thought you and Suzanne were best friends forever," Mandy continued.

Katie frowned. She was tired of hearing about Suzanne, or Ocean, or whatever her name was. "Well, now we're FRIENDS FOR NEVER!" she exclaimed loudly.

Everyone grew quiet. Katie's mother stared at her, surprised, but Katie knew her mom wouldn't say anything while Katie's friends were around.

Katie took a deep breath. She hadn't meant to sound so angry. Now everyone seemed really uncomfortable.

Katie wanted everyone to keep on having a good time. She forced herself to smile and held up her sandwich. "Here's another one for the oven, Mom."

After the cooking club had left, Mrs. Carew went outside to get the mail. She returned with a big handful of letters.

"Katie, there's one for you," she said as she walked in the door.

Katie jumped up from her seat. She *loved* getting mail. "Who is it from?" she asked excitedly.

"Suzanne."

"Oh," Katie said. "You can throw it out then."

"You don't even know what's in here," Mrs. Carew told her. She opened the envelope. "Oh, look, it's an invitation to Suzanne's modeling show. It's this Saturday at the mall."

Katie folded her arms across her chest. "I'm not going to that thing."

Mrs. Carew put her arm around Katie. "I know you're angry at Suzanne right now," she began gently.

"Her name's *Ocean*, remember?"

"That's *so* Suzanne," Mrs. Carew laughed.

Katie groaned.

"The thing is, you won't *always* be mad at her," Mrs. Carew continued.

"Yes, I will," Katie insisted.

"I doubt it," Mrs. Carew assured her. "You two have been friends for a very long time and are always having fights. And you always make up."

"Well, not this time. And I'm not going to that dumb fashion show," Katie told her mother.

"Yes, you are," Mrs. Carew said firmly. "Suzanne has worked hard in this class. You need to be there to show your support for her."

"Why?"

"Because Suzanne cared enough about *you* to invite you," Mrs. Carew reminded her.

Katie had a feeling that Suzanne's mother had sent the invitation. But she knew better than to tell her mother that. It would be a waste of time. Once Mrs. Carew made up her mind about something, there was no changing it.

Katie folded her arms and slumped back into her chair. She was going to have to go to Suzanne's dumb old modeling show.

But that didn't mean she had to like it.

Chapter 7

On Monday morning, Katie got to school just before the morning bell rang. Most of the fourth-graders were already in the yard, running around and playing tag.

Suzanne and Jessica were standing all by themselves. They were putting on lip gloss and fixing their hair.

As Katie walked by, she heard them talking.

"Dabba-id yabba-oo sabba-ee Babba-ecky's jabba-eans?" Suzanne said.

"Yabba-uck!" Jessica answered.

Katie looked at them strangely. "Did you say something?" she asked.

Suzanne shook her head. "Not to you. You

wouldn't understand."

"It's our secret code," Jessica answered. "Just for people in our club."

"So you two are the only ones who speak the language?" Katie said. She knew she was being mean, but she couldn't help it.

Jessica ignored Katie. Instead she turned her attention to Ms. Sweet, who had just walked onto the playground. "My mom gave me a note to give to *our* teacher," she told Suzanne. "I'll be right back."

"We're the only two members of the club for now," Suzanne told Katie as Jessica ran off. "But we've invited other people to join."

"You have?" Katie asked. "Who?"

"No one you know," Suzanne admitted. "We've sent invitations to all the top modeling agencies. We want real models in *our* club," she explained. "I'm sorry we couldn't invite you, but we don't want kids to be members."

"But you two *are* kids," Katie reminded her.

"Only for now," Suzanne replied. "We're

growing up quickly."

Katie frowned. "Yeah, well, your new language isn't so hard. All you did was stick the sound 'abba' in after the first letter of every word."

Suzanne gasped. Katie had figured out their code!

"I know what you said," Katie continued. "You asked, 'Did you see Becky's jeans?' and

Jessica answered, 'Yuck.' You guys are really, really mean!"

"We're not mean," Suzanne told her. "We're just fashionable. Can we help it if we're so much trendier than the rest of you?" She flipped her hair and turned her back on Katie.

"I can't believe we were ever best friends," Katie snapped. "Suzanne, you and I are FRIENDS FOR NEVER!"

Suzanne turned around quickly. "I think that's a *great* idea!" she responded angrily.

"Well, at least we agree on something!" Katie said as she stormed away.

× × ×

Katie wanted to try and cool down after her big fight with Suzanne. But she wasn't going to be able to do that in her classroom. It was hot—*really hot*—inside the classroom. The air was very steamy. There were fake trees and flowers all over the place. The sounds of birds chirping and rain filled the room. As usual, something really strange was going on in there.

"Here we go again," Kadeem said with a laugh.

"I guess we aren't studying Europe in world geography anymore," Emma S. added.

"Good guess!" Mr. Guthrie exclaimed as he jumped out from behind a big plastic tree.

"Ah!" Katie gasped. "You scared me."

"There's nothing to be afraid of here," Mr. Guthrie said.

"Where's *here*?" Kevin asked. He looked up at a monkey-shaped balloon in a plastic tree.

"We're in the Brazilian rain forest!" Mr. Guthrie announced.

Katie looked up and spotted the monkey-shaped balloon in the tree. Then she saw the vines that hung from the ceiling. The room really did look like a rain forest—except for the blackboard, of course. Suddenly, she wasn't all that jealous of Suzanne and Jessica anymore. All they had was a dumb modeling

club. Katie and her class were traveling to Brazil! (Well, sort of.) She smiled for the first time that day.

"It's really hot in here," Mandy said, fanning herself. "I'm sorry I wore a sweatshirt today."

"I can fix that," Mr. Guthrie said. He reached into a big plastic bag and pulled out a pile of T-shirts. They were all different colors. Each one said *Welcome to Brazil.*

"Girls, go change in the girls' locker room. You guys can put your shirts on in here. Then we can start talking about ways you can decorate your beanbags, so you fit into the rain forest landscape."

"Boy, Slinky sure looks happy," Kevin said as he looked into the snake's tank.

"This kind of warmth is perfect for a reptile," Mr. Guthrie explained.

Emma W. laughed. "It isn't great for hair, though," she said. "Mine's getting all limp." She wiped her bangs away from her forehead.

"And mine's curling up," Emma S. added.

All that talk about hair made Katie remember Suzanne again. Katie knew exactly what she could do to get back at her for being such a snob. "We should get Suzanne to come in here," she told the others. "She hates it when her hair frizzes."

"The rain forest just isn't fashionable," Emma W. joked.

"No, but it sure is fun," Katie agreed. She took a bright pink shirt from the pile. "I love these T-shirts."

"But, Katie, those shirts aren't in style." George imitated the snooty way Suzanne had been talking lately.

"They are in class 4A," Katie answered. "Everyone's wearing them!"

Chapter 8

Class 4A's week in the Brazilian rain forest zoomed by. Before Katie knew it, it was Saturday—the day of Suzanne's modeling show.

"I have to work today," Mrs. Carew told Katie as they gulped down a quick breakfast. "And Dad's playing tennis. So I'll drop you off at the fashion show. You can meet me at the store after the show is over."

Katie nodded. Her mother was the manager of the Book Nook, a bookstore in the mall. The store was right next to Katie's favorite restaurant, Louie's Pizza Shop.

"Can I get a veggie slice at Louie's after

the show?" Katie asked her mother. "I'll have earned it by then."

"Sure." Mrs. Carew smiled kindly at Katie. "You never know, today could be more fun than you think."

"I doubt it," Katie said as she put on her jacket and headed out the door to the car.

When Katie got to the mall, she saw that a big stage had been set up in an open area. In front of the stage, Katie spotted Suzanne's parents sitting in the second row with Suzanne's little sister, Heather. Katie figured she should walk over and say hello.

"Hello," Katie said to Suzanne's parents.

"Hi, Katie," Mrs. Lock said.

"Hey there, kiddo," Mr. Lock said.

"Katieeeeeeeeeeeeee!" Heather squealed. She took her thumb out of her mouth and gave Katie a big wet kiss.

Katie grinned as she wiped the baby spit from her cheek. She'd kind of missed Heather.

"We haven't seen you in a while," Mrs. Lock said. "How do you like fourth grade?"

"It's fun," Katie said.

"Suzanne's having a good time, too," Mrs. Lock said.

"Not today, she's not," Mr. Lock reminded his wife.

Katie looked at him. "What's wrong with Suzanne?" she asked.

"She's just a little nervous, that's all," Mrs. Lock assured Katie.

"A *little*?" Mr. Lock disagreed. "She's more than a *little* nervous. This morning, she told me she'd forgotten how to walk!"

Katie giggled. "I think she meant she forgot how to walk like a model."

Mr. Lock shrugged. "She walks fine as far

as I'm concerned."

Mrs. Lock sighed. "Katie, do you think you could go backstage and talk to her? You always calm Suzanne down."

"I don't think she . . ." Katie began.

"She'd be really glad to see you," Mrs. Lock assured her. "It would be awful if she got too nervous to go on."

Katie sighed. She was still really mad at Suzanne. But then Katie thought about what her mom had said. She and Suzanne *had* been friends for a long time. Besides, she didn't want Mrs. Lock telling her mom that she had refused to help Suzanne. That would make her mom really angry.

"Okay," Katie agreed. "I'll try."

Chapter 9

Katie couldn't believe how crazy things were backstage. Everyone was running around, carrying clothes, hairbrushes, hairspray, makeup, and more!

The really little girls were with their moms. They looked kind of weird in makeup and grown-up hairstyles.

The girls who were Katie's age were all huddled together in one corner of the room. They were brushing their hair, zipping their dresses, and giggling nervously together.

The teenagers looked like real models. They were busy talking on their cell phones while they practiced walking in their high heels.

Katie looked around for Suzanne. She saw her sitting by herself in the middle of the room putting on makeup. Katie wondered why Suzanne was sitting all alone. Did she think she was better than the other models? Katie thought about walking away and leaving snobby Suzanne to herself. But Katie had promised Mrs. Lock that she would talk to Suzanne.

"Nice pants," Katie said as she walked over toward her.

"Huh?" Suzanne said, looking confused.

"I said, 'Nice pants,'" Katie repeated, pointing to the black leather pants hanging next to Suzanne's mirror. "They're really cool. You're going to look great in them."

"Thanks," Suzanne said quietly. She stared at herself in the mirror. "I don't think I can do this."

"*You're* nervous?" Katie asked her.

"I feel like there are a million butterflies in my stomach," she answered.

"You'll be great," Katie assured her. "But don't you think you should get dressed? The show is going to start soon."

Suzanne just sat there. Katie looked around at the other girls. They were all ready to go.

"Come on, Suzanne," Katie said. "You can do it!"

"Modeling is really hard work," Suzanne told her. "I don't know if I can be the best."

"You don't have to *be* the best," Katie said. "Just *do* your best."

Suzanne sighed. "You don't get it, Katie." She turned her head slightly and looked at the door. "Oh, thank goodness," she said.

"What?"

"My assistant's here," Suzanne said. "*She'll* understand what I'm going through." Suzanne stood up and waved her hands wildly. "Over here, River!"

Jessica ran over to Suzanne. "I brought your purple lip gloss," she told her.

"You're so great!" Suzanne exclaimed. She gave Jessica a big hug and leaped out of her chair. "So do you like these pants?" She held them up against her.

"They're awesome!" Jessica told her. "You're going to be the model everyone remembers!"

"Do you really think so?"

"Of course," Jessica assured her.

"Well, this *is* what I was born to do," Suzanne boasted.

Katie's cheeks turned almost as red as her hair. She was really angry. She had come backstage to be nice to Suzanne. But now that Jessica had arrived, Suzanne was completely ignoring her!

There was no way Katie was going to watch Suzanne's modeling show now. She didn't care what her mother had said!

Tears started forming in Katie's eyes. She didn't want to let Jessica and Suzanne see that they'd made her cry. Quickly, she ran to the other end of the dressing room. She saw a bathroom and ran inside. Katie locked the door so no one would bother her. Then she leaned against the wall and tried to stop the tears from falling.

Suddenly, Katie felt a cool breeze tickling the back of her neck. Within seconds, the breeze grew stronger, until it felt more like a wind than a breeze. And not just any wind.

This was the magic wind!

Before Katie knew what was happening,
the magic wind was circling wildly around
her. Katie grabbed onto the sink and held on
tight. The tornado was really wild. Maybe the
strongest it had ever been. Katie felt like she
was being blown away.

And then it stopped. Just like that. The
magic wind was gone.

And so was Katie Carew.

Chapter 10

Katie opened her eyes slowly. She blinked a few times, getting used to the bright lights that were shining on her. There was a mirror right in front of her face.

"Oh, no!" Katie exclaimed as she looked at her reflection. Suzanne's face stared back at her from the mirror!

"What's the problem, Ocean?" Jessica asked her.

Katie gulped. How could she explain that the problem was that she *was* Ocean?

"I, uh . . ." Katie began.

"Five minutes, girls," a woman called out from the front of the dressing room.

"I'd better go get a seat," Jessica said. "You have to put those pants on. Isn't this exciting? In a few minutes, you're going to be a real model."

"Exciting isn't the word for it," Katie replied slowly.

As Jessica left, Katie stared at the black leather pants. She'd never worn anything made of leather! Katie was more into jeans and wool skirts. Leather was Suzanne's type of thing.

Of course, she *was* Suzanne now.

"Hey, Suzanne, you'd better finish getting dressed," one of the teenagers called to her. "We're starting to line up."

Katie sighed. She didn't know anything about modeling, other than what Suzanne had told her. There was no way she could go out there and walk like a model the way Suzanne did. She wanted to run away and hide somewhere until the magic wind came back.

But Katie knew she couldn't do that. This fashion show was really important to Suzanne.

And as mad as Katie was at her, she couldn't let her down. She was going to have to try and be Suzanne.

"Line up, girls," the woman in the front of the room called out. "The music's starting."

Katie quickly threw on the leather pants and zipped them on the side. Then she slipped on Suzanne's high heels and hobbled over to where the other girls were standing.

"Okay, ladies," the woman said. "It's showtime!"

Chapter 11

As she waited backstage, Katie's stomach
was doing flip-flops. She peeked out from
behind the curtain. Yikes! The runway looked
really long. She hoped she wouldn't trip and
fall.

Katie watched the little girls parading in
front of the audience. Desperately, Katie
hoped the magic wind would come back. If it
returned right now, Suzanne would be herself,
just in time to go onstage.

But deep down, Katie knew that would
never happen. The magic wind never came
when there were people around. It only
showed up when Katie was alone. And that

meant Katie was going to have to go out there, in front of all those people, and model the leather pants.

"Okay, Suzanne, it's your turn," the woman who was running the fashion show said.

Katie took a deep breath. She lifted up her neck and pushed her shoulders back, trying to copy the way Suzanne had been walking in the school yard.

Then she strutted out onto the runway. It wasn't easy, since Katie had never worn such high heels before. She blinked hard as the lights blasted right into her eyes. She couldn't see a thing. Of course, that was probably a good thing. Seeing the people in the audience would be too scary.

But she sure could hear them.

"Hey," one girl giggled. "That model is wearing her pants *backward*." The crowd of kids she was sitting with began laughing with her.

Katie looked down. Oh, no! They were right. The big back pockets were in the front. Katie had been in such a hurry to get the pants on that she hadn't noticed!

"Why is she stretching her neck that way?" someone else said. "She looks weird."

"Do you see the way she's walking? It's like she's on stilts."

Soon it seemed like everyone in the audience was laughing at Katie. She blinked hard and tried to keep from crying. This was so embarrassing!

Katie knew she was supposed to smile. But she couldn't make herself look happy. She was too miserable. The high heels were starting to really hurt her feet. The lights were blinding her.

But as she turned around and headed back toward the curtain, Katie breathed a little easier. It was almost over . . .

Boom!

Just as she'd gotten back behind the curtain, Katie tripped over one of her high heels. The audience couldn't see her fall, but everyone had heard the thud. All of the models in the dressing room began to laugh.

Katie's eyes welled up with tears. She stood and ran back to the little bathroom in the corner of the dressing room. Well, she *sort of* ran. Running is kind of hard to do in high heels!

Chapter 12

Katie couldn't believe what a mess she'd made of things. Suzanne was going to be really embarrassed when she found out what had happened during the show. After all, nobody knew it had been Katie up there. Everyone in the audience thought it was Suzanne who was wearing her pants backward and walking funny.

Suzanne was definitely the model everyone would remember.

Just then, Katie felt a strong wind blowing through her hair. Katie knew right away what that meant. The magic wind was back.

The wind circled wildly around Katie. Katie

looked around for something to hold onto. Something that would keep her from being blown away. But there was nothing around. Katie shut her eyes and hugged herself tightly.

There was nothing she could do but wait for the wind to stop.

$$\times \quad \times \quad \times$$

A few seconds later, the magic wind stopped. Just like that.

Slowly, Katie opened her eyes. She looked around. She was back in the dressing room in front of the mirror. But she wasn't alone anymore. Suzanne was standing beside her.

"Suzanne," Katie said. "Are you okay?"

Suzanne bit her lip. "Yes," she said. "I mean no. I mean . . . I don't know *what* I mean. Katie? What happened? How did I get here?"

Katie didn't know what to say. She couldn't tell Suzanne what had really happened. "Well, you were at the fashion show . . ." she began.

There, at least that was the truth.

"Oh, no!" Suzanne interrupted. "My pants are on backward."

"I know," Katie said. "But . . ."

"This is the worst day of my life," Suzanne moaned. "At least I think it is. I don't know what's going on. I mean . . . I was up on the stage, I think. And then I was back here again and . . . I'm not really sure. I'm so confused."

"You were just nervous," Katie said. "People get confused when they get nervous."

"I really messed things up," Suzanne said as she began to cry. "And lots of kids from school were there. They're going to make fun of me."

"No, they're not," Katie assured her.

"Yes, they will.

They'll all be happy to make fun of me. Especially after I made such a big deal about being a model." Suzanne gave Katie a funny look. "How come you're being so nice to me? I thought you hated me."

Katie shook her head. "I was mad at you. But I could never *hate* you, Suzanne."

Suzanne shrugged. "Well, not everyone is as nice as you, Katie. Jessica was out there, and so were Miriam, Mandy, Becky, and Zoe. I invited them. What was I thinking?"

"You didn't know that . . ." Katie began.

"I think I even heard George laughing in the audience!" Suzanne sobbed. "I'm going to be the joke of the fourth grade. I'm never going to model again!"

"Don't say that," Katie pleaded. "You'll do great next time."

Suzanne shook her head. "There won't be any next time."

Chapter 13

That night, Katie lay in her bed. She felt awful. She might have been mad at Suzanne, but that didn't mean she had wanted to ruin her modeling career.

But that's exactly what Katie had done. And what was worse, Katie knew Suzanne was right. The kids in school *were* all going to make fun of her.

And it was all Katie's fault.

Katie stared at the ceiling. There had to be some way she could help her friend. But how? There was so much the kids could laugh about. Suzanne had been holding her head funny and walking like a man on stilts. Worst of all, she'd done everything with her pants on *backward* . . .

That was it!

Katie had just gotten one of her great ideas!

✕   ✕   ✕

On Monday morning, Katie arrived at school extra early. She was wearing a striped pink-and-green sweater, and her new green corduroy pants. But . . .

She was wearing the pants backward!

Emma W., George, Becky, and Mandy were the first people to see Katie.

"Katie," Emma whispered to her. "Your pants are on backward."

"I know," Katie said proudly. "They're supposed to be that way."

The kids looked at her strangely.

"Suzanne wore them this way in her fashion show," Katie said.

Becky giggled. "I remember."

"It was classic," George added.

"*You* were there?" Mandy asked.

"I was on my way to Louie's," he said quickly, making sure the girls knew he hadn't gone to the mall to see Suzanne. "I passed the stage just in time to see Suzanne looking ridiculous."

Katie shook her head. "She wasn't ridiculous at all. That's the way all the big fashion models are wearing their pants now."

Becky and Mandy looked at her strangely. "Yeah, right. Anyway, we thought you were still mad at her."

"Well, that doesn't mean I don't trust her fashion sense," Katie replied.

"I think your head's on backward," George told Katie.

Before long, a whole crowd of kids had gathered around Katie. She was determined to make the whole fourth grade think wearing your pants backward was in style.

"You guys know Suzanne would never have worn her pants backward by mistake. She's too into fashion to do something like that," she told them.

"But your pants look weird backward," Miriam Chan told Katie.

Katie shrugged. "Lots of fashionable stuff looks weird. How about models who wear rings on their toes? Or male models who carry those man pocketbooks?"

The kids all looked at one another. It was

hard to argue with logic like that.

"I should have known Ocean was wearing her pants that way on purpose!" Jessica said finally.

"Well, I'm going inside to turn my pants around," Miriam declared.

"Me too," Emma S. said.

"I can't believe I wore a skirt today," Becky moaned. "I wish I had pants I could wear backward."

And then, Suzanne arrived. Everyone stared at her in surprise.

Suzanne wasn't wearing *her* pants backward. She was wearing a plain jeans skirt, a polo shirt, and flat blue shoes. She wasn't wearing any earrings, bracelets, or necklaces. She didn't have any glitter anywhere.

"Check out Suzanne," Kadeem said. "She looks so *normal*."

"Suzanne is never normal," Jeremy reminded him.

"Well, she *looks* it," Kadeem reminded him.

Katie felt awful. Suzanne without glitter was the saddest sight in the world. She hurried over to the bench where Suzanne was sitting all alone.

"Hi," Katie greeted her.

"Hello," Suzanne said in a quiet voice.

"You okay?"

Suzanne shrugged. "I guess." She looked down at Katie's green corduroy pants. Her eyes got really small and angry. "I can't believe you're wearing your pants that way. I thought you were my friend."

"I am," Katie assured her.

"Then why are you making fun of me?"

"I'm not," Katie promised. "I'm wearing my pants this way *because* I'm your friend. I did it so no one would be mean to you."

Suzanne looked at her strangely. "Huh?"

"I told them you said *all* the top models are wearing their pants this way."

Suzanne smiled. "And they believed you?"

Katie nodded. "They figured if *you* were wearing clothes this way, it had to be a fashion trend." She pointed to Miriam Chan, Zoe Canter, Emma W., and Emma S. They had all just come out of the school building. And their pants were on backward!

Suzanne looked down at her plain, boring outfit. "But now everyone will know you were lying."

Katie frowned. She hadn't counted on Suzanne coming to school dressed like that.

Suzanne thought for a moment. "Unless maybe I . . ."

"What are you going to do?" Katie asked her.

Suzanne grinned. "You'll see. You're not the only one with great ideas, Katie Kazoo."

Chapter 14

By lunchtime, most of the girls in the fourth grade were wearing their pants backward. But not Suzanne. She was still wearing her jeans skirt and plain shirt. Only the shirt wasn't so plain anymore. It had a big glittery *S* on it. Her pocketbook had an *S* on it, too.

"How'd you do that?" Katie asked as she stood beside her best friend in the lunch line.

"Glitter glue," Suzanne answered. "It was easy."

"How come you didn't put an *O* for Ocean?"

Suzanne frowned. "I think I like Suzanne better. It's a French name, did you know that?"

Katie smiled. "I like Suzanne better, too,"
she said.

Suzanne's glittery letters caught the
attention of the girls in the fourth grade.

"Suzanne, how come you're not wearing
backward pants?" Miriam asked her.

Suzanne sighed dramatically. "Backward
pants are so last Saturday. Today, everyone's
wearing initials. Check the fashion magazines.
You'll see."

The girls all sighed. Once again, Suzanne's fashion trends were moving faster than they were. She was ahead of them again.

In seconds, there was a crowd of girls standing around Suzanne. They listened intently as Suzanne talked about how she painted the glitter glue letters on her clothes.

Katie moved out of the way and left Suzanne in the center of the crowd. She took her tray and sat down alone at a quiet table in the corner.

A minute later, she heard a familiar voice behind her. "Is it okay if I sit here?" Suzanne asked.

Katie looked up, surprised. She and Suzanne hadn't eaten lunch together in a long time. "Sure."

Suzanne smiled and sat down beside her. "Katie, I'm really sorry about being so mean. I guess I got kind of weird about this whole modeling thing."

"Kind of," Katie agreed. "But it's okay."

She paused for a minute. "I just have one question, though. How come you picked Jessica as your assistant and not me?"

"Oh, that's easy," Suzanne said. "An assistant works for you. But I could never be your boss, Katie. You're my best friend."

Katie smiled. Now she understood.

"I mean, I *hope* we're still best friends," Suzanne added nervously.

"Of course we are," Katie assured her happily. "You and I are friends *forever*!"

Blizzard Fruit Salad

Suzanne and Jessica were at the next Cooking Club meeting. Here's the snack Katie and her pals made. Katie's mom did all the cutting. You should get an adult to help you with that, too.

Ingredients:

$1/2$ watermelon sliced the long way

1 cup cantaloupe balls

2 oranges sliced and peeled

1 large sliced banana

1 cup seedless grapes

$1/2$ cup pineapple tidbits

$1/2$ cup raspberries

$^1/_2$ cup blueberries

1 cup shredded coconut

1 cup oranges

1 tablespoon sugar

1 tablespoon cinnamon

Directions: Scoop out the watermelon half. Cut the watermelon into chunks. Combine the watermelon chunks and the rest of the fruit in a large bowl. Mix in the rest of the ingredients, except the coconut and cinnamon and sugar. Pour the mixture back into the watermelon shell. Mix the cinnamon and sugar together, and sprinkle it throughout the mixture. Then top the fruit with lots of snowy, white coconut.